STORIES FOR A

Fragile Planet

To Evi and Kati   K.S.
For Gillian and David   J.R.

A Lion Children's Book
an imprint of
Lion Hudson plc
Wilkinson House, Jordan Hill Road,
Oxford OX2 8DR, England
www.lionhudson.com
Hardback ISBN 978 0 7459 6157 6
Paperback ISBN 978 0 7459 6386 0

First hardback edition 2010
3 5 7 9 10 8 6 4 2
First paperback edition 2012
1 3 5 7 9 10 8 6 4 2 0

Typeset in 16/21 Venetian 301 BT
Printed in China July 2012 (manufacturer LH06)

Distributed by:
UK: Marston Book Services Ltd, PO Box 269, Abingdon, Oxon OX14 4YN
USA: Trafalgar Square Publishing, 814 N Franklin Street, Chicago, IL 60610
USA Christian Market: Kregel Publications, PO Box 2607, Grand Rapids, MI 49501

STORIES FOR A
Fragile Planet

Kenneth Steven

Illustrated by Jane Ray

LION
CHILDREN'S

CONTENTS

How the Seasons Came to Be

In ancient times, the Greeks wondered about the world and why things happened as they did. Their legends told of gods, each of whom had charge over some part of the world. This is the story of Hades, god of the underworld, and his love for the beautiful Persephone. It is the story of how the seasons came to be.

Many gods and goddesses of ancient Greece had their home at the top of Mount Olympus; others lived in the sky or sea, or in the deep forests. Mighty Zeus ruled over them all.

But one god lived deep underground, far from the beauty of the upper world. His name was Hades and he was the king of the underworld. In that dark land, the sun never shone, nor did a single bird sing. It was the place of the dead, and the only sound was that of silence.

"I am lonely," Hades thought to himself. "I am king of this underworld, but what happiness does it bring me? More than anything, I long to have a wife. I will ask Zeus if he will let me marry Persephone."

Now, Persephone was the daughter of Demeter, and Demeter was the goddess who gave life to every leaf and branch – and everything that grew. She would never allow her daughter to marry a god like Hades.

But Hades had fallen in love with the beautiful Persephone. He thought about her night and day, trying to work out a way she could become his wife and come down to live with him in the dark sadness of the underworld. Zeus knew of Hades' longing, and finally he decided to help him win Persephone.

One magnificent day, Persephone was gathering flowers on a hillside. The air was full of birdsong and the chattering of a stream as it danced down to the valley below. Persephone's heart was filled with happiness; she would gather as many flowers as she could pick for her mother and take them home as a gift.

All at once, the earth broke open with a terrible roar. A black chariot pulled by black horses raged upwards, and in her terror Persephone fell backwards, the flowers tumbling from her hands. Hades, his face grim and

cold, reached out one steel arm to grab Persephone, dragging her into the chariot and down into the ground to his underworld. The earth closed over them and the quiet returned. The sun that had gone into darkness now shone on the pile of scattered flowers poor Persephone had left behind.

When Demeter found out what had happened, she hurried to Mount Olympus to find Zeus.

"My daughter has been stolen by Hades," she wailed. "Will you let my heart break in two? I am the one who gives life to all things that grow, but how can I give that life when I am filled with sadness and anger? I cannot, not until my beloved girl returns from Hades."

In the valleys, the grass began to wither. Nothing grew in the fields; the land turned bare and grey. Children cried because there was not enough food for them to eat. Day after day, nothing but a bitter wind hissed, and the people huddled in their homes and shivered. When would it ever end? Down in the underworld, Persephone wept and pleaded with Hades.

"Please let me go back to where I belong. I cannot be happy here where there is only darkness and silence. How can I give you happiness when there is none left in me?"

But Hades kept his back turned to Persephone.

Zeus knew this could not go on. The people of earth were dying because of Demeter's rage and grief. Down in the underworld, Hades saw the suffering of the people on earth and knew he could not keep Persephone a prisoner any longer.

"You may go back, Persephone," he told her. "Forgive me for thinking you could live here in my dark world. I was a fool for believing that. Go back and be happy in the sunlight and the beauty of the world above."

Persephone did not need to be told twice. She ran up and up through the dark caves until at last her eyes were filled with the bright light of the day. She skipped and sang for joy; she did cartwheels as she laughed once more.

"My beloved girl!" Demeter cried as she saw her, and they embraced in the morning light. But as she looked at her daughter, she saw a strange darkness on her lips. Fear leaped into her heart.

"Did you eat anything down there, Persephone? Please tell me that you didn't!"

Persephone looked at her mother, not understanding.

"Only six pomegranate seeds," she said. "Hades gave them to me. I was so unhappy he made me eat something. But that was all I would have."

Demeter buried her face in her hands. She knew Persephone had been tricked by the king of the underworld, for whoever eats down there in the darkness must go back there.

So, ever since, Persephone has had to go back to Hades' underworld for a time. For one part of the year she is with her mother and the earth rejoices – the trees spread their leaves, the birds sing, and the skies are blue. But then Persephone has to say goodbye and go back to the silence of the underworld. Demeter weeps and the earth lies desolate and grey. But that is the natural pattern of the year, and there is no other way it could be.

THE HUNTER AND THE SWAN

Hunting has been part of how humans make a living since the beginning of time.
However, this story from the Far East is about a hunter who loved killing for its own sake
and how in the end he was confronted by his actions.

One day in early autumn, a hunter went out to shoot birds. There was not so much as a breath of wind, and the world was beautifully calm. Mist lay like wool in the valleys, but up above, the sky was as pure and blue as a cut sapphire. But the hunter did not notice the lakes that lay as still as mirrors; he had no eyes for the forest paths. All he heard was the jangle of the arrows in the quiver at his shoulder. His heart thudded with the thrill of the hunt.

It wasn't long before five great swans flew overhead. It was so still, he could hear the whirring of their wings. The long white necks of the swans stretched out almost as if they swam through the morning sky.

An arrow thrummed upwards from the hunter's bow. It arched and caught the sunlight as it rose and rose; as it fell it clipped the wing of one of the swans, and down came both arrow and bird. They fell into the deep trees, so far ahead of the hunter that he could not see precisely where they had come down. But he started searching.

It so happened that a young girl was carrying water home from the well when the swan landed close to her, the arrow tangled in its wing.

The girl ran to the bird. She loved everything that lived in the forest: she knew where the otters played in the river pools; she could get close to the deer as they grazed. She hated to see any living thing suffer, and now her heart grieved when she saw the swan.

She reached out to the bird as it lay helpless on its side. She had once nursed a bird with an injured wing, and she knew how to hold it so she could not hurt it more. She pulled the arrow very carefully from its wing. Finally the swan was free, but red blood stained its magnificent white feathers.

The girl dipped her hands into the clear water of her bucket. She carefully washed the swan's wing and gently laid on it special leaves she had found on the edge of the clearing, and which her mother had taught her brought healing.

Just then, two very different men came into the glade from opposite sides of the forest. One was the hunter, red-faced and out of breath. The other was a holy man who often came to that glade to pray.

"Give me my swan!" the hunter shouted angrily when he saw the girl

crouching beside the bird. "I shot it and it's mine!"

The girl didn't move. But the holy man came forwards and stood between the hunter and the girl.

"That's not true," he said quietly. "A living thing belongs more to the one who gives it life than to the one who tries to take it away. You wanted to kill the swan; this girl has done all she can to heal it."

The holy man bent down, picked up the arrow, and handed it back to the hunter.

The man was red with rage, but he could find no words to speak.

Finally he stormed off into the trees, the quiver rattling against his shoulder.

The holy man smiled and bent down to look at the swan's wound.

"You did well," he said to the girl. "One day, the swan will fly once more."

THE SAINT AND THE BLACKBIRD

This story comes from the days of the Celts who lived on the eastern shore of the Atlantic. It tells of a man who loved every living creature around him, and of how he put the life of one single bird above his own comfort.

Once there lived a special man by the name of Kevin. In fact, it's because of him the name is so popular today. His home was in Ireland, in a wild and lonely place where the waves came in from the sea huge and fierce, and where a wind blew all the long year. But Kevin loved his home, and he went out every day to a small shelter under the hill where he could pray to God and thank him for his creation.

For Kevin knew all the birds and animals and they knew him too. He knew where the seals came out of the water and lay on the rocks to sing their strange songs, and he had given a name to every skylark that sang up on the moorland above the little shelter where he lived.

So it was that Kevin was out early one spring morning to pray. The mist was rising from the fields and, up above, the hills were covered with a scattering of snow. There wasn't so much as a breath of wind – it was going to be the most beautiful day.

Kevin came to his special place of quiet in the rocks and knelt down, stretched out his arms, and cupped his hands. He closed his eyes to pray, to thank God for all the great beauty of the world, for all the wonderful things he had created with such love and care.

At that moment, a blackbird spied his hands. She had been searching for a place to build her nest since the first moment of light that morning. Now she noticed the cupped hands Kevin stretched out into the air – they would be a place of warmth and safety for the laying of her eggs! She flew down so softly and nestled in Kevin's cupped hands with such little movement that he didn't even notice she was there.

It wasn't until a whole hour later, when he opened his eyes and was about to stand up to return to his shelter, that he caught sight of her at last.

"What a wonderful thing!" he whispered to himself. "This blackbird has trusted me so much that she has chosen my hands for her nest!"

But soon Kevin began feeling hungry and cold. He realized it would be many days before the blackbird's eggs had hatched. Would it really be possible to wait that long in such a cramped position? Kevin was almost in despair. He prayed that God might help him and give him an answer, for the last thing he wanted was to move and disturb the bird.

And then he heard voices, and his name being mentioned! It was his two dearest friends, who had chosen that very day to come and visit him. They listened as he explained the whole story to them and then they smiled and shook their heads, for they well knew Kevin's love for all God's creatures, large and small.

"We'll stay and see you have everything you need," they promised, and brought a blanket for his shoulders and warm food for him to eat. When night fell, they made sure he was comfortable to sleep. Day after day

they looked after him with kindness, as any good friends would do. Kevin kept so still that each morning a doe and her fawn came to drink from a stream close by. They were so close to him and the nesting blackbird that he could hear their breathing.

One day, Kevin felt the eggs cracking. His heart was filled with joy as he thought of the young birds alive on the palms of his hands. The mother bird flew back and forth with food for them, just as Kevin's friends brought all he needed, day after day.

"I could never have done this without you," he told them. "God sent you to find me at just the right moment."

They were all there early one morning when the three young birds stretched their wings and flew – the first, the second, and then the third. The mother blackbird sat on a rock and sang a song of thanks to Kevin for all the love and goodness he had shown.

The Tale of the Lion

The lion is said to be the king of the jungle. This tale comes from Africa and tells how one lion lost his strength, then found it once more.

All through the night the wind howled in the African savannah, and much had been destroyed. In all the villages it was the same. Everywhere people woke up to find their goats and sheep wandering among the broken fences. The people had to begin the task of clearing up.

But one man who had lost a calf was determined to find it. He began to search in every corner of the valley and saw no sign of it. He started to climb up into the foothills of the mountains. Soon he would have to give up and go back home, but not yet. He knew there was little chance now that he would find his calf; it would never have wandered so far. His heart was heavy. But just as he was about to accept defeat, what should he see beside a rock but a young lion cub! It must have strayed from its mother and was now hungry and frightened. The man was in two minds. He knew very well that lions attacked cattle, but this young cub would die if it were left abandoned. In the end, he picked it up, and began the long walk back to the village.

When he returned, all the children crowded around him, full of excitement to see a real lion cub. They gave him the good news that his missing calf had come back to the village safe and well that morning. The man set down the cub with some of the puppies and soon it was playing and rolling with them as if it were just another dog. It ate their food and drank their water.

The weeks and months went by. One of the man's friends came to visit the village. He laughed when he saw the young lion.

"That lion thinks like a dog and acts like a dog," he said. "It will never become a real lion."

The man was annoyed. He threw a stick into the air and the lion leaped with the young dogs and rolled with them in the dust, trying to catch it.

The next day, the man's friend was laughing again.

"Look at that lion!" he exclaimed. "It's as soft as butter!"

The man's friend went over to the lion, who rolled over, stretched out its paws, and let him stroke its tummy. The cub purred so loudly that the other villagers came out of their homes and laughed too. The man who had found the lion felt very annoyed, but he had no idea what to do or say.

All that night, he couldn't sleep. He lay awake, listening to the breeze in the trees, and he wondered. He lay awake thinking about the lion he had found all those months ago. Long before dawn, he made up his mind. He got up, dressed, found a lantern, and went to find his friend.

"Come on," he said. "I know it's early, but I want you to come with me."

The man found his lion sleeping with the dogs and he woke it up too. The lion trotted at his heels as they went out into the valley.

They walked and walked until the grass gave way to stones. They began to climb uphill, into the foothills of the mountains. The man's friend was very puzzled. Why on earth were they there so early in the morning? What was the reason for being there at all? Everything was dark and silent around them. The cold shadows of the rocks loomed on every side. The path became steeper all the time. Their feet were sore and their steps slow and careful.

It felt strange and dangerous climbing such a steep mountain in the dark. But the lion found its way up the path without the slightest difficulty. It seemed to know every step of the way.

At last they were close to the summit. Both men were out of breath and freezing cold. The wind came in gusts and the ledge where they stood was narrow. One slip and they would fall.

But now there was a greyness to the sky. They could see rocks and trees and the valley down below, although they were still vague and shadowy. And up above the men, right on the very top of the mountain, was the young lion.

When the first light of morning came from the east, it was like a fire of gold and crimson. The two men had to cover their eyes. But above them, the lion opened its mouth and roared. Now it was a young cub no longer. It had come back to where it belonged and it was a puppy no more – it was a lion. With a fierce snarl it leaped from the rock, bounding down and down the steep slope towards a herd of springbok grazing far below.

And the man who had once rescued it smiled. He turned to his friend.

"The lion needed to come home," he said. "It had to remember where it belonged."

Grey-eye and the Whale

*The Greenlanders have many, many legends concerned with their seas and its creatures.
This one is about the first European people who came to their icy
island to hunt.*

A long time ago in Greenland, a little girl called Grey-eye lived with
her mother and father in a tiny cabin at the edge of the sea. Every
day, summer and winter, she went down among the rocks to a place from
where she could look out over the waves and icebergs to the great backs of
the whales as they rose into the air and plunged back into the deep. Grey-
eye loved the whales and had names for every one of them.

But this particular night she had a strange dream. She saw great white
birds skimming across the sea and all the water turning a deep and
terrible red. In her dream, Grey-eye was crying. She woke up full of fear,

and although her parents comforted her, she still felt afraid of all she had seen in her nightmare.

Not long afterwards, Grey-eye was sitting as usual in her favourite place beside the water's edge. It was sheltered there, out of the wind, and it was her place and no one else's. That day it was so clear that she felt she could see right across the sea. To Grey-eye's horror, she suddenly saw great white birds skimming over the water towards her, just as she had dreamed. Except they weren't birds at all, but ships with white sails.

Grey-eye wasn't the only one to see the ships. Everyone from the village close by had heard about her nightmare and they now gathered everything they needed and got ready to leave their homes. They had decided that they would go up into the hills and hide in their summer shelters, for they were now full of fear themselves. They carried the young children in their arms, and the dogs barked around their feet.

"I'm going to stay here," Grey-eye told her parents. "You go on without me – I promise I'll be careful and keep safe."

Her mother and father tried to persuade her to come with them, but in the end they knew it was useless. Grey-eye had to stay behind and remain close to the sea she loved so dearly, with all its wonderful creatures. Her mother and father said goodbye and followed the others up into the hills.

The men in the great white ships hunted the whales and killed them. The sea turned red, and Grey-eye knew this was her nightmare coming true. They went on killing the whales until the ships were loaded and they could carry no more. Then they set sail and headed south, out of the Greenland Sea.

Grey-eye had watched from her secret hiding place. Now, when the last ship had left, she knelt down in front of the sea and wept. Her heart was broken by the killing of all those wonderful creatures. She was filled with such sadness that she cried all through the night, her tears forming a stream. The stream grew and became a little river; it flowed through the rocks and out into the sea – the river of Grey-eye's tears. For a night and a day she wept, and for a night and a day the river of her tears flowed into the sea.

When she stopped crying at last, she saw that all the people were coming back. She could hear their voices as they talked and the barking of the excited dogs. Her family joined her and her mother held her close. She looked out again over the sea that had been red with blood and saw that it was red no longer.

Something wonderful had happened to the Greenland Sea. Grey-eye's tears had filled it with salt, and because of her salty tears, new creatures came to swim there. Walruses with great thick skins appeared, and there were narwhals, like unicorns with their beautiful white tusks. Hundreds and hundreds of seals came to swim around the rocks and islands in the bay, for the salty sea was teeming with fish – every fish you could think of.

And now and again, a sleek, dark back arches through the sea and a tail flickers in the light. For Grey-eye's beloved whales are there again too, and the Greenlanders say it was her tears that made the sea the way it is today.

A Fishy Tale

In Russia, there are almost as many folktales as there are fish in the sea.
This is one of them, in which the main character has the strangest of meetings.

A man and his wife were very poor and lived in a tiny cottage in the countryside in Russia. They were too cold in winter and too hot in summer. They had one hen, one sheep, and a thin cat called Matushka, and when the sheep wasn't bleating or Matushka wailing, then it was the wife who was shouting about how little firewood they had or how hard the bread was. All in all, it was hardly a quiet place, and as the cottage only had one main room for all five of them, there weren't many corners to hide in.

So sometimes the man went fishing. He told his wife that he was getting fish for dinner, but he wasn't usually very good at fishing, and what he was really doing was escaping from a noisy home. On the river bank, all he could hear was birdsong. He could forget about all the things they needed.

"Don't come back until you've caught a fish!" his wife shouted. That was fine by him. He sat by the river bank all morning and all afternoon, and in the end he felt a lot better about life and was happy to shuffle back home through the woods humming to himself, even though he had little to show for his efforts and was bound to receive a telling off.

"What! Just one tiny trout! That won't even feed Matushka!"

One day, he was almost ready to go home and still hadn't caught a thing. All at once, he felt a small tug on the line. It was a tiny gold fish, unlike any other he had seen before. It was so small that he didn't have the heart to take it home to eat. He was about to throw it back into the water when the fish suddenly cried out.

"Stop! Because of your kindness, I want to grant you a wish!"

The man almost fell into the river with shock. Never in his whole life had he heard of a talking fish! It took him a minute to recover before he could think of anything to wish for.

"I suppose I'd wish for a bigger house," he said at last. "An extra room for the animals, please."

Well, the man went home with no fish, dreading what his wife was going to say. But when he got there, he found that she was busy sorting out their furniture because now they had two rooms instead of just one. So the wish had come true after all! The man was so excited that he decided he would tell his wife what had happened, but instead of being happy, she went red with rage.

"You stupid man! You had the chance to wish for whatever you wanted and all you could think of was one extra room! What about a nice cottage like our neighbours have and a whole flock of sheep instead of just this one maggoty beast? Go on – get moving and find that fish again!"

The man went back to the river and searched and searched until he had found the fish. He explained that his wife wanted a much bigger house, a summer cottage, and a garden. In the end it sounded much more like a shopping list than a wish.

"All right. You'll find things just the way she wants them."

The man thanked the fish and went back home in the moonlight. He hardly recognized the place where they lived. All of it looked very grand, but half the woods had been cut down to make way for the house, the cottage, and the garden. The family of squirrels that had lived in the glade had gone, and the pond where all the frogs had been was covered over now with the grass for their lawn. The man went into his elegant new house with a heavy heart.

But his wife saw none of that. She mumbled and grumbled and was as dark as a thunderstorm. Where were some decent clothes for her to wear, and why couldn't there be a proper woodshed to store their winter fuel in? What about a new road to town so the journey wouldn't be so bumpy? The man went back and forth to find the little gold fish, and every time his wife's wish was granted.

But he used to enjoy watching the bear cubs playing in the forest, and the coming of the new road had scared them away. All the building work had made the stream that ran past the house a funny colour, and the beavers didn't make their dam there any more. The man sat by the stream one evening and thought to himself that his wife wasn't any happier than she used to be, and he was definitely miserable.

"The only thing that's going to make me content is to be in charge of everything!" his wife shouted the following morning. "Go and tell that fish to make *that* come true!"

The man went off as usual to find the fish. The wood was silent; there wasn't a single animal, and no birds sang. All he could hear was the sound of his own footsteps. He realized that he felt lonely.

But this time the fish sounded very sad.

"I'm sorry, but that's a wish I can't grant. That's impossible. I'm afraid she will never be content – no wish is ever enough."

The fish disappeared and the man turned for home. But when he got close to their grand new house, he saw instead in front of him just a tiny hovel, with a hen and sheep and a thin cat beside it. The man listened and realized that the birds were singing again, and the stream was flowing just as it used to. And over on the other side of the stream, he could make out the shapes of the bears as they played in the long grass. He smiled, because his wish had been granted that everything might be just the way it once had been.

His wife appeared in the doorway, and to his surprise she didn't look angry, nor was she shouting or unhappy. Instead, there was a very shy smile on her face.

"I'm sorry," she said quietly. "I know I was greedy and we're poor again, but now I see what good things we have all around us. I'll try not to grumble any more."

THE PANDA'S TALE

Giant pandas are very precious to the Chinese people, who love them and try to look after them. This story tells of children who did everything they could to help one panda in trouble.

Three sisters lived close to the great mountains and forests of China. They were good friends and loved walking together in the forest beside their village. They loved the living things they saw there: brightly coloured woodpeckers, banks of spring flowers, and the shadows of wild animals. This was a place where all kinds of treasures of nature were to be found.

"Let's go walking," the eldest sister said early one morning. "The snow's almost melted now and it's going to be a beautiful day."

But they wrapped up warm because it was still not quite spring.

They decided they would walk to the river and then go on into the forest until they could see the highest mountains. How wonderful they would look with snow on their peaks!

They said goodbye to their mother and father, and started along the path towards the first trees. They were very quiet so as not to scare any birds or animals; they whispered together and pointed out things to each other as they walked. Soon they heard the roaring of the river ahead of them. It was so full of melted snow that the ground shook beneath their feet.

"Look! What's that in the water?" the youngest shouted, completely forgetting to be quiet. She had seen something struggling close to the bridge. The three of them started running as fast as they could. Whatever the creature was, it was very big.

"It's a bear!" they exclaimed together.

Sure enough, the black and white creature in the water was a giant panda. The girls knew they lived in the mountains, but pandas were rare and they had never seen one before. But this panda was in trouble. It had been crossing the half-frozen river and fallen in. Now its thick fur was soaked with freezing water and its paws were slippery and numb. It couldn't climb out from the river without help.

The girls looked at each other in dismay. They'd promised to come home quickly and they knew that if they didn't, their parents would start to worry. But they had to help the panda! What on earth were they to do?

The eldest made the decision for them.

"Listen," she said to her smallest sister. "Run back home and tell our parents that we're all right. Explain what's happened and that we need help!"

At once, the youngest nodded and set off, swift as the wind.

"Come on, I have an idea how we might rescue the bear," the eldest said to the middle sister. "But we have to hurry!"

The two girls looked all around. Over in the shadows was the trunk of a fallen tree. The bear needed something to catch hold of! Between them, they carried the trunk to the river until they were above where the bear was struggling to get out. Very carefully the eldest sister went down close to the edge of the bank. They lowered the trunk until one end was under water and secure. But would the panda have the strength to hold on?

The eldest girl scrambled up the bank to stand beside her sister. Then the panda saw. Its great paws reached out towards the trunk and it began to climb.

But it seemed to take for ever, all the same. The bear slipped back into the water and had to begin again. The sisters could see the poor animal was tired. But it didn't give up. The great arms reached up once more to hug the trunk and slowly it began to haul itself out, little by little. At last, the bear clambered up onto the bank!

Suddenly the girls heard shouting. Their parents were running down towards them, with their sister leading the way. Behind them came villagers carrying great bundles of bamboo. They collected sticks to build a fire beside the river to warm the freezing panda. They had brought other food too – boiled meat and rice and sugar – and they fed the panda very carefully to restore its strength.

At first the panda just wanted to sleep, but finally it began to take an interest in the food. The heat of the fire dried the animal's thick fur until

at last it could struggle onto its feet once more.

The three sisters were so happy. They held hands and watched as the great creature rambled back into the forest, safe and well. It turned around once and blinked, as if to thank them for all they had done to save its life.

MAHA AND THE ELEPHANT

A tsunami is a giant wave. It has a Japanese name because in the past terrible
mighty waves have hit the Japanese islands and destroyed everything in their path.
This story is about a tsunami, but it comes from Thailand. What happened is true, but
the story is told through the eyes of someone imagined.

Maha had gone to Thailand because of the great beauty of the
sea there. There are many shades of green in that water, and
they shimmer like painted jewels. Out in the deep waters of the sea are
wonderful, strange islands. They are like green pillars, rising on tall stilts
of rock, but covered with trees on top. The water laps beaches that curve
for miles and miles – beaches made of the finest white sand.

Sometimes Maha swam here all day, for the water was beautifully warm
and clear. But on other days, he preferred to hire an elephant and ride

up the jungle paths into the cool of the forest. The elephant's great grey feet made almost no sound at all on the paths, so the birds and butterflies weren't frightened away. Maha believed that by the end of every day he had got to know his elephant. He was certain that they were wise creatures and that each one listened and watched and understood.

On this day, the day of the story, Maha was with a group of other travellers on the beach. They were swimming and laughing, talking about everything they had done and seen in the last few days. That evening they were going to make a fire on the beach and bring their guitars to sing together, for all of them loved music.

Maha turned and saw the elephants at the top of the beach, standing chained beside their owners as usual. He recognized the one that had taken him into the jungle two days before. But why were they making such a noise? They were trumpeting and stamping, waving their trunks wildly from side to side. The mahouts, the men who looked after them, were trying to calm them but they weren't succeeding.

On the other side of the beach there was another group of elephants, and it was just the same with them. It was as though they were trying to say something, Maha thought. It was as though they knew something the humans didn't. But what could it be?

The friends on the beach decided to investigate. They got out of the water and went towards the nearest group of elephants. As they got closer to them, the elephants became even more frantic. The young elephant that had

taken Maha into the jungle recognized him and reared up, trumpeting.

The chain that held the elephant's foot broke.

"I think they're warning us!" Maha shouted to the mahouts. "I think they want to tell us something and try to help us!"

A mahout nodded and began releasing the elephants from their chains. He helped Maha up onto the young elephant's back, and at once it began chasing away from the beach towards the jungle and the hillside. All of Maha's friends and the mahouts did the same, and all of the other elephants followed Maha's elephant as fast as they could, up and up into the jungle. They didn't trumpet any more; they made no noise at all. They climbed the path to a level piece of ground and there they stopped.

Maha looked out over the sea. What was that strange line in the water? It was rising and coming closer and closer. The others were watching too,

but no one said a word. It was a giant wave, a tsunami. The elephants had known the wave was coming; they had sensed it long before it could be seen.

The wave grew into a great tower of water. It spilled onto the beach and snapped the trees. It crashed up and on in a terrible roaring, higher and higher until it was just a little way from the elephants. The beautiful jewelled birds scattered in terror; every living thing fled for its life.

Maha reached out to touch the face of the elephant that had recognized him and saved his life. He leaned forwards to put his head gently against that wise, great head. There were no words he could find for his gratitude. The elephants had saved them from the tsunami.

THE SHEPHERD AND THE STONE

*Humans have always dreamed of finding precious stones. This story from
South America tells of one such stone and the high price that was paid for it.*

In the mountains that stretch down South America like a spine, a
shepherd found a jewel. He simply came across it when he was bringing
his flock to new pastures. He did not know what it was he had found,
but he knew the stone was special. He held it up to the early morning
sunlight and it flashed like living fire.

He put it into the folds of his cloak and forgot all about it until the
day he met the merchant in the village. The merchant gave him a few
small coins for it. The merchant sold the stone to a trader and the trader
showed it to the governor. The governor took it straight to the king, who
smiled.

"I want you to open up a mine in the mountains where the shepherd found this, for I am sure there will be many more stones there like this one," he said. The king held the stone to the light and it flashed like living fire.

But a deep forest lay between the sea and the mountains. A road had to be built so that wagons with miners and tools and rocks that were dug out of the mountains could come and go. The road had to be as straight as an arrow and as wide as a river. The air was filled with the sound of splintering wood as the ancient trees were hacked down one by one. And the creatures of the forest, the jaguars and the giant otters, the condors and the mountain lions, fled in terror. The road cut the forest in two like the blade of a knife.

Then the miners came and began digging into the mountain. They hacked at the rock and dug tunnels deep into the darkness. But the strange thing was that they didn't find many of the beautiful precious stones after all. There were a few, and some of the miners became very rich indeed, but most went back home to their villages when there was no more mountain to dig, and they stayed just as poor as they'd always been. The road lay silent and empty, cutting the forest in two.

One day, the shepherd who had found the beautiful stone came over the mountain and saw the empty road in front of him. He had been away for a long time and had not heard anything about the mine. The road was a white scar through the forest and he wept with sadness to see it. But he

had no idea it had been made because of the one little stone he had once found. Now the mine was abandoned and the road was empty and silent: there was no need for it any more. The shepherd was so angry that he went down to his village and called together all the children.

"I want each of you to find me a hundred acorns and cones and nuts," he said to them. "It's autumn and there are plenty all around. And I want you to tell your friends in other villages to do just the same – to gather a hundred each and bring them all to me."

The children scattered in every direction. Day after day, the shepherd found the pile of seeds and cones growing taller and wider. The children enjoyed the task and were happy to tell others to help too.

The shepherd worked with the children. Every day he walked along the road, the folds of his cloak full of nuts and seeds. He scattered them across the road and pressed them into the ground with his crook. Every day, he went to a new place with as much as he could carry, and every day, when he came home, the pile of seeds and cones was as high as it had been before.

At last they ran out of road and there was nothing left of the pile to scatter. That evening it began to rain. The lightning flickered like snakes' tongues in the sky and the thunder growled like bears. The rain sang from the skies, and in the silence of the earth, the new things grew. In a year, the road could barely be seen; in ten, it was forgotten. The forest was cut down the middle no longer, and all the wild creatures and birds returned, one by one.

THE STORY OF THE TOWER

The Bible book of Genesis tells of Babel, a tower that was built to reach the sky.
This is an imaginative retelling of the Bible story, seen through the eyes of
a child of the time.

It is now so long since all of this took place, but I can think back to that time as clearly as if it were yesterday. I am an old woman and I do not remember many things that I should remember, but how could I forget this, the biggest story of my life?

I look out of the window of this tiny, simple house and hear the tinkling of animal bells as the flocks and herds wander near and far. It was no different back then when I was a child of just four years of age.

This land is beautiful; I love it with all my heart. Everything we could want is here for us between the two great rivers: refreshing water and rich soil for our corn. In summer, the air is full of butterflies and everywhere is turned to purest gold. God has been good to us indeed, but we have not always understood that or been wise to his ways.

I well remember the day my father came into this very house and called his children, excitement in his voice and his eyes shining.

"Come and look! Come and see the tower they are building! The tower that is going to reach the sky!"

We ran outside into the early evening light and my father lifted me onto his shoulders so I could see properly, for I was the smallest of his children and always seemed to be at the back, pushed out of the way.

Even today I can picture it: the golden light of the setting sun, the distant glittering of the rivers, and a tower rising into the sky. Even though we were far away, we could hear the sounds of shouting as the men worked. They looked as small as ants, hundreds and hundreds of them talking and arguing and laughing together. I felt so excited.

One day, we begged my father to take us to see the great tower close up. He was a kind man and it did not take long to persuade him. My eldest brother agreed to stay behind to look after the animals, and early the next morning we set off.

The tower had seemed small from a distance, but as we walked, it rose taller and taller into the sky. There was such a crowd all around! People who had loved their fields and animals had left them behind to come to work on the great tower. It was the only thing in their minds. Nothing else seemed to matter except this!

"Once upon a time, we believed in God," my father said as we huddled around him. He had to shout because of all the noise. "Now we think we are like gods. There is nothing we cannot do!"

But I can remember feeling frightened by the great tower. It was like some huge creature reaching into the sky. I could barely see the top of it when I tilted back my head.

I awoke with a jump the next morning, feeling strangely fearful. It seemed to me that the calls and shouts among the workers were louder than usual. They were angrier too, and soon I heard chanting and booing.

Not long afterwards, a gang of several hundred workers came marching down the path that wound past our home. They were all chanting together, but I couldn't understand the words they were using.

Next came another group – this one with a different chant using words I did not know. When they reached the river path, they turned in a different direction from the first group.

And so it went on. Within just a few days, all the workers had left. They went in every direction, and later I heard they had gone to seek their fortunes in new places. The tower was left as it stood, silent and unfinished. I did not understand then, but I think I do now.

My father believed that it was all God's doing. He had told us that we thought we were like gods; there was nothing we could not do. We had become too arrogant; we thought we did not need God any more.

I do not know exactly what happened at the tower. I was only a child then, and we lived a long way away from the building. But what I do know

is that God showed us he is more powerful than we are; try as we might, we humans will always argue and fall out. We talk in different ways, and we do not understand each other.

All that was a long time ago. The tower was never finished. Instead, the bricks began to weaken and crumble in the wind and rain, and started to fall. Even to this day, without warning, bricks may fall, and none of us dares go too close.

But we are still here, with our flocks and the land we love with its flowers and seasons and wild creatures. It is a simple life we lead, but we have everything we need.